TULSA CITY-COUNTY LIBRARY

W9-CFE-587

When I Am Old with You

Story by ANGELA JOHNSON   Pictures by DAVID SOMAN

ORCHARD BOOKS   NEW YORK

Text copyright © 1990 by Angela Johnson
Illustrations copyright © 1990 by David Soman
All rights reserved. No part of this book may be reproduced or transmitted in any form or by
any means, electronic or mechanical, including photocopying, recording or by any information
storage or retrieval system, without permission in writing from the Publisher.

Orchard Books
95 Madison Avenue, New York, NY 10016

Manufactured in the United States of America.
Book design by Mina Greenstein.
The text of this book is set in 18 pt. ITC Caslon 224 Book. The illustrations are watercolor
paintings reproduced in full color.
Hardcover 10   9   8
Paperback   18   19

Library of Congress Cataloging-in-Publication Data
Johnson, Angela. When I am old with you / by Angela Johnson ; illustrated by David Soman.
p.   cm. "A Richard Jackson book." Summary: A child imagines being old with
Grandaddy and joining him in such activities as playing cards all day, visiting the ocean,
and eating bacon on the porch.
ISBN 0-531-05884-0.   ISBN 0-531-08484-1 (lib. bdg.)
[1. Grandfathers—Fiction.   2. Old age—Fiction.]   I. Soman, David, ill.   II. Title.
PZ7.J629Wh   1990   [E]—dc20   89-70928   CIP   AC

To my parents, Arthur and Truzetta

A. J.

To my grandma
for a lifetime of love and support

D. S.

When I am old with you, Grandaddy,
I will sit in a big rocking chair beside you
and talk about everything.

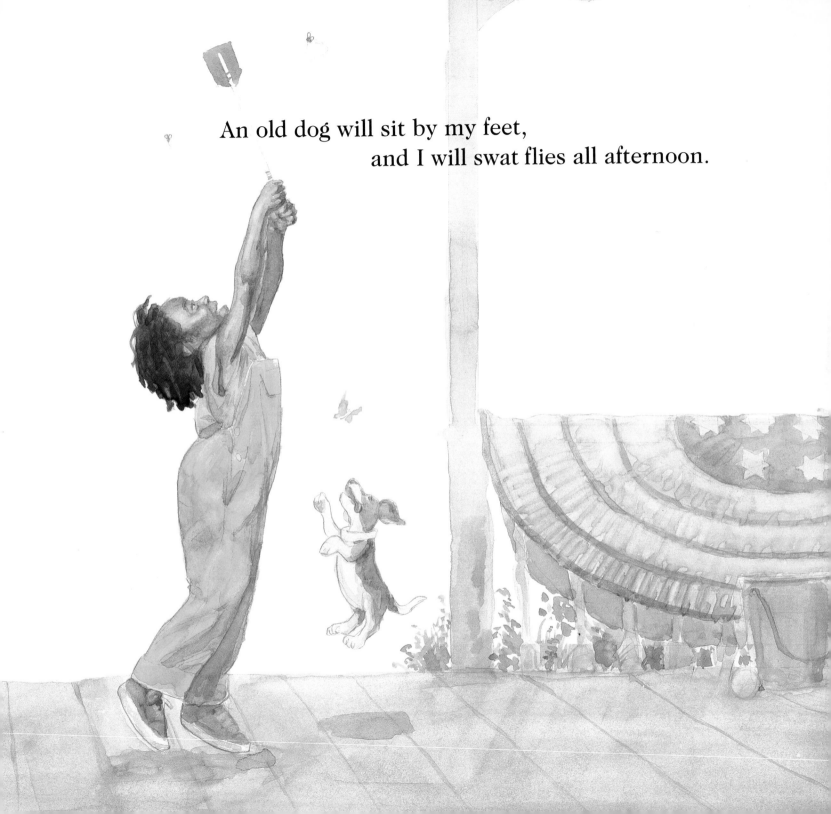

An old dog will sit by my feet,
   and I will swat flies all afternoon.

We'll go fishing too, Grandaddy, down by that
old pond with the flat rocks all around.

We can fish beside the pond or take that old canoe out.

We'll eat out of the picnic basket all day and we won't catch any fish…

…but that's all right, Grandaddy.

When I am old with you, Grandaddy, we will
play cards all day underneath that old tree by the road.

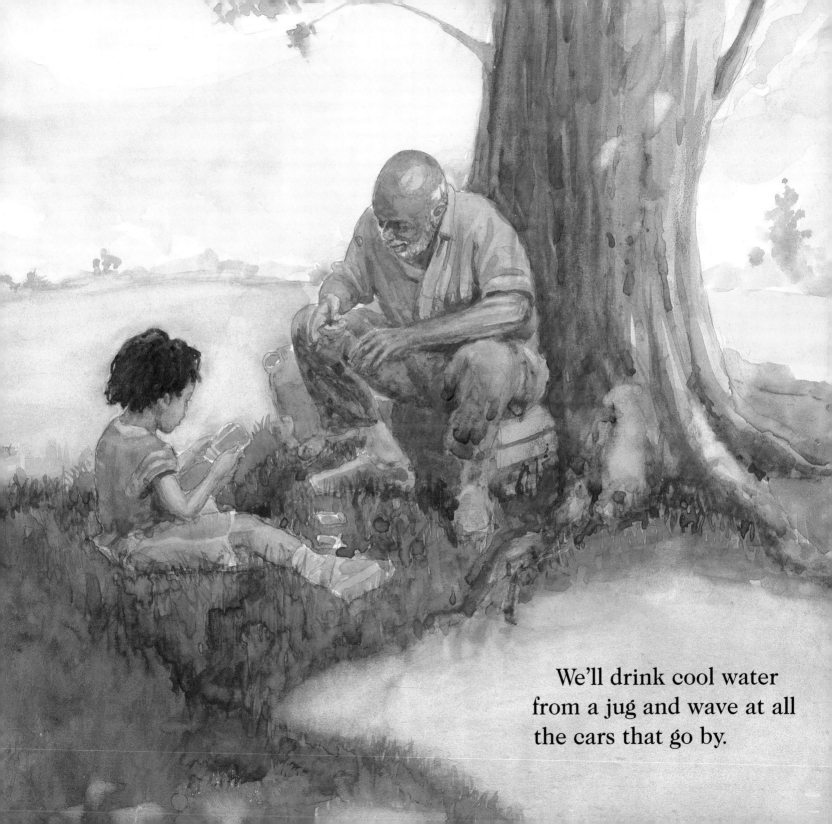

We'll drink cool water
from a jug and wave at all
the cars that go by.

We'll play cards till the lightning bugs shine
in the trees…
…and we won't mind that we forgot to keep
score, Grandaddy.

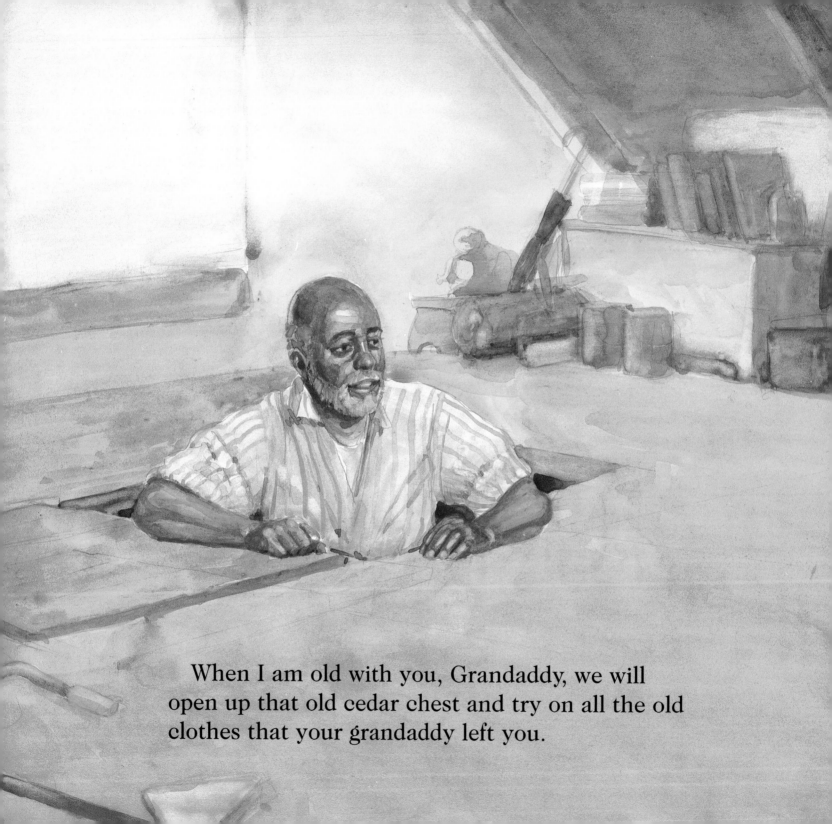

When I am old with you, Grandaddy, we will open up that old cedar chest and try on all the old clothes that your grandaddy left you.

We can look at the old pictures and try to imagine the people in them.
It might make us cry…
but that's O.K.

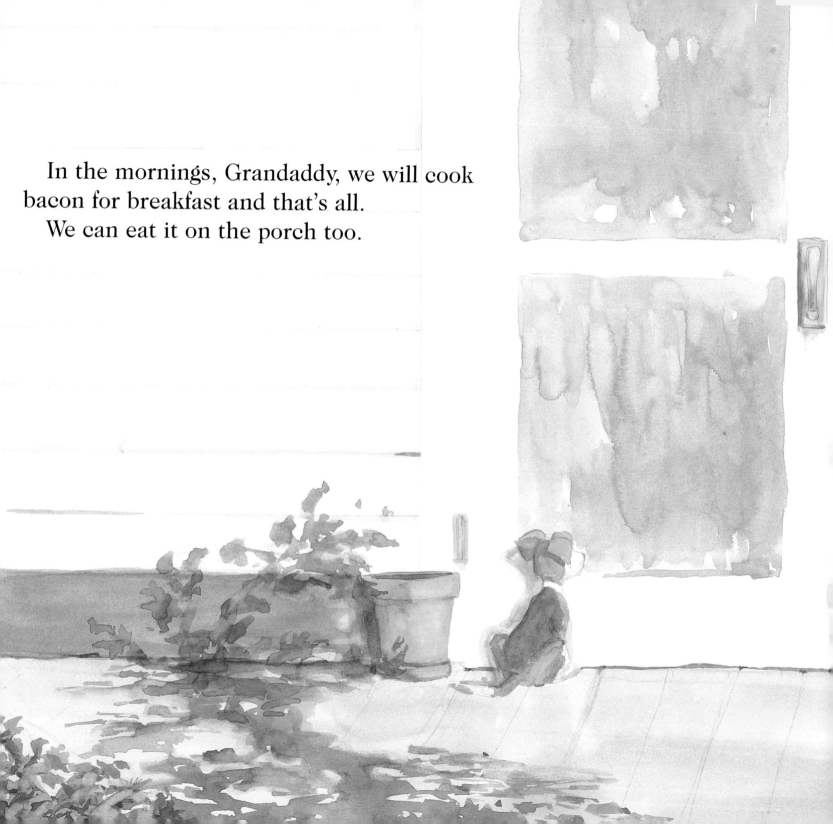

In the mornings, Grandaddy, we will cook
bacon for breakfast and that's all.
We can eat it on the porch too.

In the evening we can roast corn on a big fire and invite everyone we know to come over and eat it. They'll all dance, play cards, and talk about everything.

When I am old with you, Grandaddy, we can
take a trip to the ocean.
Have you ever seen the ocean, Grandaddy?

We'll walk on the hot sand and throw rocks at the waves.

We can wear big hats in the afternoon like everyone else…

…and we'll sit in the water when the day gets cool.

When our trip is over we will follow the ocean as far as we can, so we'll never forget it.

When I am old with you, Grandaddy, we will get
on the tractor and ride through the fields of grass.

We will see the trees in the distance and remember when this field was a forest.

We won't be sad though.

Grandaddy, when I am old with you we will take long walks
and speak to all the people who walk by us.
We'll know them all, Grandaddy, and they'll know us.

At the end of our walk, when we're tired,
Grandaddy, I will sit in a big rocking chair...
beside you.